CELEBRATE SCIENCE

MOLE AND TELL

WRITTEN BY **CATHERINE PAYNE** AND **JOHN PAYNE II**

ILLUSTRATED BY **ELISA ROCCHI**

Science, Naturally!
An imprint of Platypus Media, LLC
Washington, D.C.

Celebrate Science: Mole and Tell
Hardcover first edition • May 2023 • ISBN: 978-1-958629-11-6
Paperback first edition • May 2023 • ISBN: 978-1-958629-10-9
eBook first edition • May 2023 • ISBN: 978-1-958629-12-3

Written by Catherine Payne and John Payne II, Text © 2023
Illustrated by Elisa Rocchi, Illustrations © 2023

Project Manager, Cover and Book Design: Marlee Brooks, Chevy Chase, MD
Editors:
    Caitlin Burnham, Washington, D.C.
    Hannah Thelen, Silver Spring, MD
Editorial Assistants:
    Caitlin Chang, Amara Leonard, Sienna Sullivan, Tristan Tanner

Coming soon in Spanish.

Teacher's Guide available at the Educational Resources page of ScienceNaturally.com.

Published by:
    Science, Naturally! – An imprint of Platypus Media, LLC
    750 First Street NE, Suite 700
    Washington, DC 20002
    202-465-4798 • Fax: 202-558-2132
    Info@ScienceNaturally.com • ScienceNaturally.com

Distributed to the book trade by:
    National Book Network (North America)
    301-459-3366 • Toll-free: 800-462-6420
    CustomerCare@NBNbooks.com • NBNbooks.com
    NBN International (worldwide)
    NBNi.Cservs@IngramContent.com • Distribution.NBNi.co.uk

Library of Congress Control Number: 2022944460

10 9 8 7 6 5 4 3 2 1

To our mother who encouraged our love of reading, and to our father who sparked our passion for science.
— Catherine Payne and John Payne II

To my son, Leonardo, my curious little boy.
— Elisa Rocchi

A Letter from the Authors

Dear Reader,

Our childhood home in Guam and our first science laboratory were one and the same. The kitchen experiments we did when we were young sparked a fascination with science that never died out. Understanding scientific concepts can be scary at first, but this book about moles will serve as your own metaphorical lab to explore science and indulge your quest for knowledge.

We hope that you see yourself in these characters and know that anyone can contribute to a better world through imagination, scientific discovery, and a handful (or a mole!) of curiosity. We are honored to have written this book for you, our young readers, whose boundless excitement will one day improve lives in immeasurable ways.

Happy reading!

Catherine

John

Catherine Payne

John Payne II

The students filed into Mr. Cantello's science classroom, still out of breath from recess.

"What is that date written on the board?" Leilani asked.

Akiko looked at the board. "Do we have a field trip coming up?"

10/23

"No, not a field trip," Mr. Cantello answered. "October 23rd is a special science holiday. Can anyone guess which one?"

"Is it Astronomy Day?" Fatima asked. "I want to be an astronaut when I grow up."

"Close! Astronomy Day was a couple of weeks ago. Anyone else?"

6

"I hope it's Earth Day!" Kevin exclaimed. "I love when we plant seeds in the school garden."

"That's not until spring. One more guess."

"Pi Day!" Sanjay shouted. "My family always eats pie on Pi Day."

"Good try, Sanjay, but Pi Day is in March," Mr. Cantello smiled. "October 23rd is Mole Day, which celebrates a unit of measurement called a mole. What do you think moles measure?"

Before anyone could guess, Kevin called out, "Wait! A mole isn't used to measure something. A mole is an animal."

"It's also a spy who works undercover. I saw it in a movie," Alejandro added.

"No, a mole is a colored spot on your skin!" Leilani said. "I have one right here."

"That's true, Leilani, a mole is a spot on your skin. It can also be a spy and an animal," Mr. Cantello said. "The word 'mole' is a homonym, which means that it has more than one meaning. Today, we will be learning about the kind of mole that is used by scientists."

"A mole is a universal unit of measurement," Mr. Cantello explained. "This means that scientists all over the world—from Brooklyn to Buenos Aires to Beijing—use moles to measure things."

"So my cousin who lives in Japan would understand moles too?" Akiko asked.

"Exactly!" Mr. Cantello said. "Even though scientists may speak different languages at home, they all have a common scientific language so they can understand each other and work together."

11

"What do moles measure?" Kevin asked.

"Chemists use moles to measure really, really small things like molecules, particles, and itty bitty atoms. They are so small that you can't see them, even with a microscope."

"But, Mr. Cantello, what *is* a mole?" Sanjay asked.

"A mole is a counting unit in the same way a dozen is," Mr. Cantello answered. "When you have a dozen of something, like eggs or donuts, it means that you have 12. When you have a mole of something, like atoms or molecules, it means that you have around 602 billion trillion."

"Wow, that's a big number!" Fatima said.

"Yes, it is, but there's a way to shorten it," Mr. Cantello began to explain. "Who here has a nickname?"

Alejandro raised his hand. "Sometimes my family calls me Al."

"Why do you think they do that instead of always saying Alejandro?"

"I guess because it's shorter and easier to say," Alejandro shrugged.

602,000,000,000,000,000,000,000=6.02×10²³

"Exactly! Just as you can simplify a long name by using a nickname, you can simplify really long numbers by using scientific notation. It makes numbers easier to read and easier to say out loud," Mr. Cantello said. "The way to say this big number in scientific notation is six-point-zero-two times ten to the twenty-third, and you write it like this: 6.02×10^{23}."

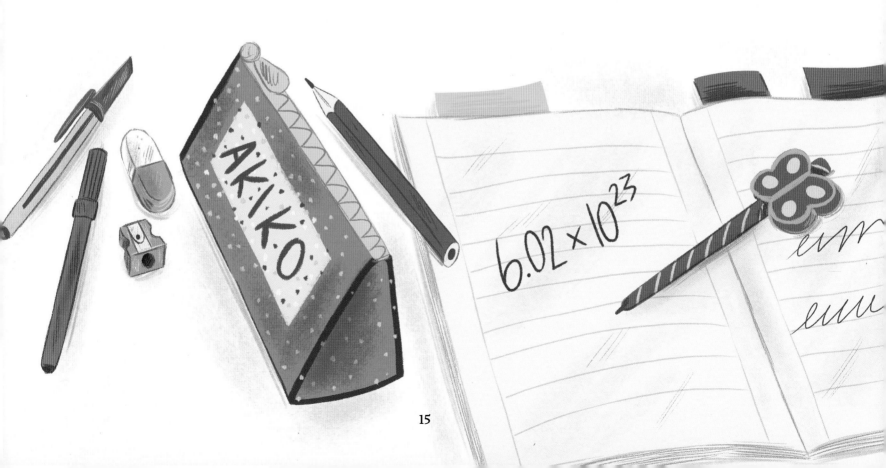

"That nickname is much easier to remember than those billions," Leilani said.

"Mr. Cantello, where did this number come from?" Alejandro asked.

"The mole was discovered by an Italian chemist named Amedeo Avogadro," Mr. Cantello told the class.

"Avocado?" Akiko asked.

16

"No, Avo-*gadro*," Mr. Cantello laughed. "He studied molecules, which are groups of atoms that stick together. His research led to the development of the mole. In fact, people even call the mole Avogadro's number."

Amedeo Avogadro

Turin, Italy 1776-1856

"Moles are so important that scientists all around the world celebrate International Mole Day from 6:02 a.m. to 6:02 p.m. on October 23rd," Mr. Cantello told the class.

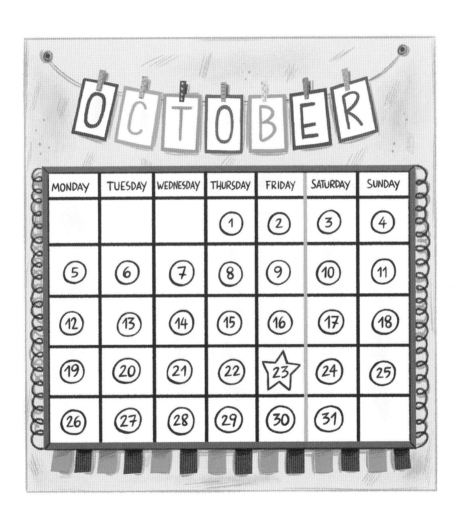

"I get it! October is the 10th month of the year, so 6:02 and 10/23 are pieces of Avogadro's number," Fatima said.

"Exactly," Mr. Cantello nodded. "This year, all of you young scientists are going to join the festivities."

"That's this Friday," Sanjay said. "How are we going to celebrate?"

"We're going to have Mole and Tell!" Mr. Cantello answered.

"Mole and Tell?" Akiko asked. "What's that?"

"Each of you will share a fun fact about moles to help us learn more about them and why they are so important."

"Where do we find mole facts?" Fatima asked.

"Ask your friends and relatives what they know about moles, or research them on the internet," Mr. Cantello said. "You can even bring in one mole of something to show the class."

Friday in Mr. Cantello's Classroom...

"Good morning, everyone. Welcome to our first ever Mole and Tell," Mr. Cantello grinned. "Who wants to go first?"

Fatima raised her hand and walked to the front of the class. "I brought one mole of water. My mom helped me figure out that it's only 18 grams."

"Good work, Fatima," Mr. Cantello said. "It's hard to believe that there are 602 billion trillion water molecules in that bottle!"

"Hold on..." Kevin said in confusion. "Why does my mole of sugar look so much bigger than Fatima's mole of water?"

"That's because moles tell you the *number* of molecules you have, not the *size* of them," Mr. Cantello said.

"Imagine that you have a dozen donuts and a dozen donut holes. Even though there are 12 of each, the donuts are going to take up more space than the donut holes because they're bigger.

"The same thing is true with moles. One mole of sugar takes up more space than one mole of water because sugar molecules are bigger than water molecules."

"Ohhh," Kevin said, "I get it now!"

"Who would like to share next?"
Mr. Cantello asked.

"I will!" Alejandro said. "I did some research on Mr. Avogadro, and I found out that it actually took a whole bunch of scientists to finalize 6.02×10^{23} even though the number is named after only one person."

"Nice job, Alejandro. Scientists usually work together to make discoveries, just like when we work together on projects in class," Mr. Cantello explained. "Most discoveries are group efforts that come from years of teamwork, even if they are named after just one person."

H Hydrogen															B Boron	
Li Lithium	Be Beryllium															A Alumi...
Na Sodium	Mg Magnesium															A Alumi...
K Potassium	Ca Calcium	Sc Scandium	Ti Titanium	V Vanadium	Cr Chromium	Mn Manganese	Fe Iron	C Coba...		...pp...	Zn Zinc	G Galli...
Rb Rubidium	Sr Strontium	Y Yttrium	Zr Zirconium	Nb Niobium	Mo Molybdenum	Tc Technetium	Ru Ruthenium	Rh Rhodium	Pd Palladium	Ag Silver	Cd Cadmium	I Indi...
Cs Cesium	Ba Barium		Hf Hafnium	Ta Tantalum	W Tungsten	Re Rhenium	Os Osmium	Ir Iridium	Pt Platinum	Au Gold		T ...alli...
Fr Francium	Ra Radium		Rf Rutherfordium	Db Dubnium	Sg Seaborgium	Bh Bohrium	Hs Hassium	Mt Meitnerium	Ds Darmstadtium	Rg Roentgeni...		

La Lanthanum	Ce Cerium	Pr Praseodymium	Nd Neodymium	Pm Promethium	Sm Samarium	Eu Europium	Gd Gadolinium	Tb Terbium	Dy Dysprosium	Ho Holmiu...
Ac Actinium	Th Thorium	Pa Protactinium	U Uranium	Np Neptunium	Pu Plutonium	Am Americium	Cm Curium	Bk Berkelium	Cf Californium	Es Einstei...

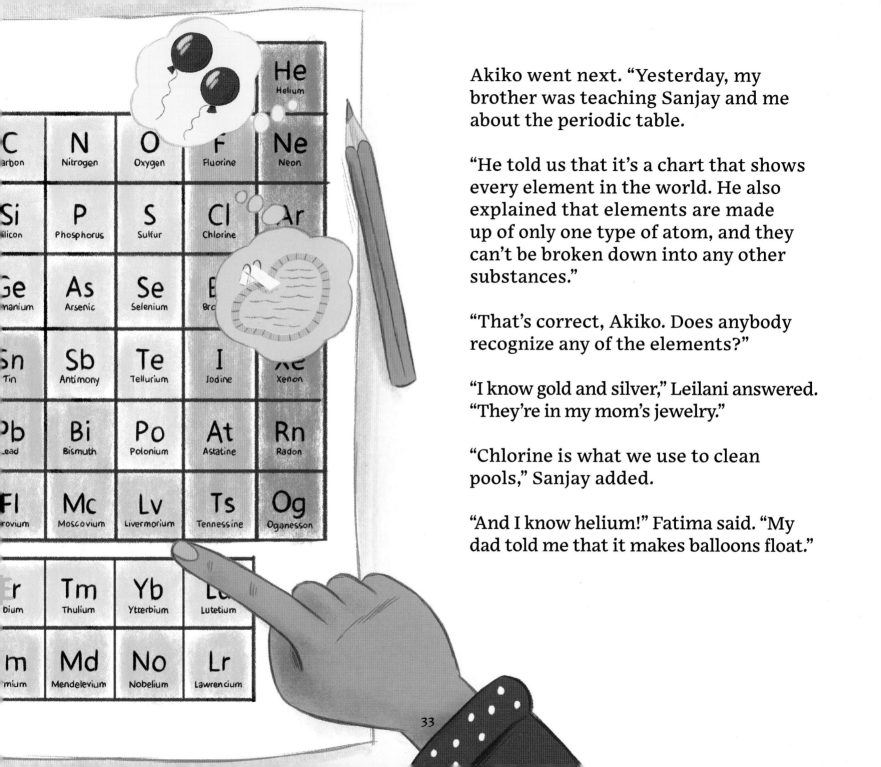

Akiko went next. "Yesterday, my brother was teaching Sanjay and me about the periodic table.

"He told us that it's a chart that shows every element in the world. He also explained that elements are made up of only one type of atom, and they can't be broken down into any other substances."

"That's correct, Akiko. Does anybody recognize any of the elements?"

"I know gold and silver," Leilani answered. "They're in my mom's jewelry."

"Chlorine is what we use to clean pools," Sanjay added.

"And I know helium!" Fatima said. "My dad told me that it makes balloons float."

"That's right!" Mr. Cantello said. "All of those substances—and lots more—are elements on the periodic table, which is universal, just like the mole. Scientists all over the world use the same periodic table."

"Akiko's brother taught us something else about the periodic table," Sanjay said. "He told us that each element has a number at the bottom of its box called molar mass. Molar mass tells you how many grams there are in one mole of that element. That means one mole of gold is about 197 grams."

"That's right, Sanjay." Mr. Cantello said.

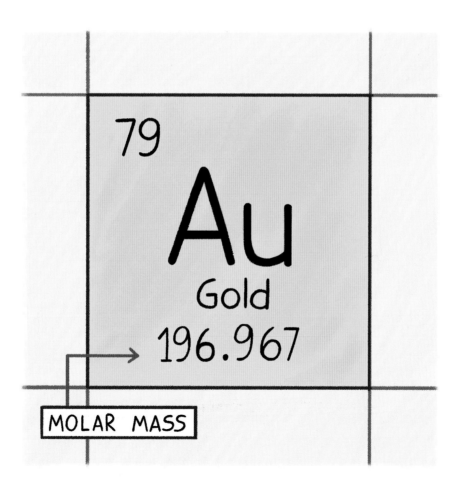

Leilani went last. "My mom is a pharmacist. She uses moles at work to measure chemicals for different medicines."

"A lot of people use moles for their jobs," Mr. Cantello said. "Scientists who make plastic and batteries have to measure specific amounts of different elements when they create their products. In many cases, they use moles to take these measurements."

"Wow," Alejandro said. "Moles are everywhere!"

"They are," Mr. Cantello said. "That's why it's so important for us to learn about them."

"You all did such a great job with today's assignment. Now I have one 'mole' surprise." Mr. Cantello brought out a plate of pastries. "In honor of our favorite Italian scientist, Mr. Avogadro, I made *zeppole* donuts. *Buon appetito!*"

Kevin raised his hand. "Mr. Cantello, which science holiday are we celebrating next?"

Amedeo Avogadro – the Italian chemist most famous for his work with gas molecules that led to the discovery of the mole. His work—along with many others—determined a standard unit for measuring large quantities of very small things.

Atom – the smallest unit of an element. Atoms are the basic building blocks of chemistry and they make up everything in the universe—even you!

Element – a basic substance made of one type of atom that cannot usually be broken down into a simpler substance. Gold, helium, oxygen, and calcium are examples of elements.

Molar Mass - the mass (similar to weight) of one mole of a substance, measured in grams. On the periodic table, an element's molar mass is displayed at the bottom of each box.

Mole – a unit used in chemistry to measure the amount of a substance. One mole of molecules is about 602,000,000,000,000,000,000,000 (also written as 6.02×10^{23}) molecules. According to the National Institute of Standards and Technology, one mole contains exactly $6.02214076 \times 10^{23}$ molecules.

Mole Day – the holiday that commemorates Avogadro's number each year on October 23rd, celebrated from 6:02 a.m. to 6:02 p.m. This holiday was created to spark interest in chemistry and is observed in schools across the country.

Molecule – a group of atoms bonded together. For example, a water molecule is a bonded group of two hydrogen atoms and one oxygen atom.

Periodic Table – the scientific chart that displays all chemical elements.

Scientific Notation – a method of simplifying very long numbers into short numbers by multiplying a number between 1 and 10 many times. In a mole, 10 is multiplied by itself 23 times and then multiplied by 6.02.

Substance – a type of matter, such as an element or combination of elements, that has specific chemical properties.

AUTHORS and ILLUSTRATOR

Catherine Payne worked as a journalist after earning master's degrees from Harvard and Columbia Universities. After returning to her native Guam, she became an English instructor and tutor. Catherine especially loves writing books that transport children to happy places. The inspiration she draws from Pacific cultures helps her appreciate the interconnectedness of all things. Contact her at Catherine.Payne@ScienceNaturally.com.

When **John Payne II,** Catherine's brother, discovered superhero comic books, it sparked a lifelong love of reading that led to an interest in speech and language. After pursuing degrees at San José State University and the University of Hawai'i at Mānoa, John now works with kids as a speech clinician in Guam. Contact him at John.Payne@ScienceNaturally.com.

Elisa Rocchi grew up in the countryside of northern Italy, along with her unique friend and pet cat, Minù. She has always loved drawing and writing and works as a children's book illustrator. Elisa currently lives in Milan, Italy with her husband and son. To see more of Elisa's work, visit ElisaRocchi.it.

RESOURCES

National Mole Day Foundation
American Chemical Society
Amedeo Avogadro, Famous Scientists
Amedeo Avogadro, Britannica Kids
National Institute of Standards and Technology

Teacher's Guide at ScienceNaturally.com
YouTube: International System of Units by
   Laboratoire national de métrologie et d'essais
YouTube: How Big is a Mole? by Daniel Dulek
YouTube: What is a Mole? by Extraclass